The Magic Garden FROG

Shann Jones and Hannah Rounding

For the real Macsen, Isabella and Elis,
who brought the real magic into my garden.

This book belongs to:

____

____

____

GRAFFEG

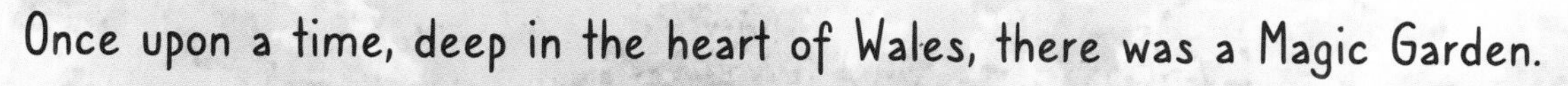

Once upon a time, deep in the heart of Wales, there was a Magic Garden.

Mamgu looked after the garden, and her three grandchildren, Isabella, Elis and Macsen, loved to come and play there.

Everything in the garden was round. There were round glass domes full of fruits and flowers, and a circle of trees all the way around the garden.

There was a round gate at the top and another round gate at the bottom and, in the middle of the garden, there was a beautiful round fountain, encircled by stones.

One day, the grandchildren were exploring the garden when they saw a frog in the fountain! The frog had dark green skin and beautiful big brown eyes that were looking right at them. The children ran inside.

"Mamgu, we found a frog in the fountain!" they said.

Did you know that when frogs swallow something, they have to close their eyes? This is because their eyeballs go down into their mouths to help them swallow!

ISA
MACS
LIS

"That's wonderful!" Mamgu said. "Frogs are great helpers in the garden, because they eat lots of slugs and bugs that can harm my flowers. Let's build the frog some steps so that she can easily get in and out of the pond."

They built the steps, and even made a cosy house with leaves on top.

The children stayed down by the pond all afternoon, watching the frog. They named the frog Suki. Suki was basking on a rock that sat just below the water, with only her head poking out. Then, suddenly, Suki flicked out a long tongue at them – once, twice, three times! The children felt a funny tingly feeling all over.

They were all shrinking! With a splash, they fell into the fountain. Wriggling around, they realised that they could swim. Not only that, but they could breathe underwater!

"What are we?" said Elis.

"I think we're tadpoles!" said Macsen.

"I like being a tadpole," Isabella laughed.

"Hello, children," said Suki, appearing beside them. "Welcome to the fountain."
Did you know that baby frogs, or tadpoles, are born with gills like a fish and can only live underwater? They can't breathe air until they get older.

"Hello, Suki!" they said. Close up, they could admire the handsome black spots on the frog's back. "Come and take a look around," Suki said. They followed, swimming easily with their new oval heads and long tails.

There were floating plants under the surface like trees, and caverns to explore and play in. Whenever they got hungry, Suki showed them how to eat algae off the side of the pond. It was delicious and tasted just like cake!

Did you know?
Once hatched, tadpoles take about 14 weeks to transform into tiny frogs.

After a few weeks, Tadpole-Isabella started growing lungs. "That is so that you can breathe air when you're a grown-up frog," said Suki.

Then Tadpole-Macsen grew a pair of legs next to his tail! It made swimming even faster.

A week after that, Tadpole-Elis grew a pair of front legs as well. "Now you're a froglet," said Suki. "You're growing up."

Did you know that adult frogs can breathe through their skin, as well as through their lungs?

The frog-children were used to living in the pond now, swimming through the sparkling water and basking in the warm sun. Suki taught them many things – how to use their legs to jump, how to catch insects with their tongues and how to croak beautiful songs at night.

Did you know that frogs are amazing jumpers? A frog can jump 20 times its own body length, whereas a human can only jump about three times its body length.

One day, Suki gathered them on the flat rock where they had first met.

"You're grown-up frogs now," said Suki, "and you must go back to the human world."

The children didn't want to go, because they loved living in the fountain with Suki.

"I'll tell you a secret," said Suki, looking at them with beautiful, sad eyes. "Frogs like us are in danger. Every year, fewer frogs are born. But you can change that. When you go back to the human world, you can make it your mission to care for all the precious creatures of this world. Use your human hands to look after them, with all the love in your heart."

Did you know frogs are one of the most ancient groups of animals on Earth? Frogs first appeared on our planet about 250 million years ago, during the age of the dinosaurs. Now we must all work together to make sure that these wonderful creatures are protected for the future.

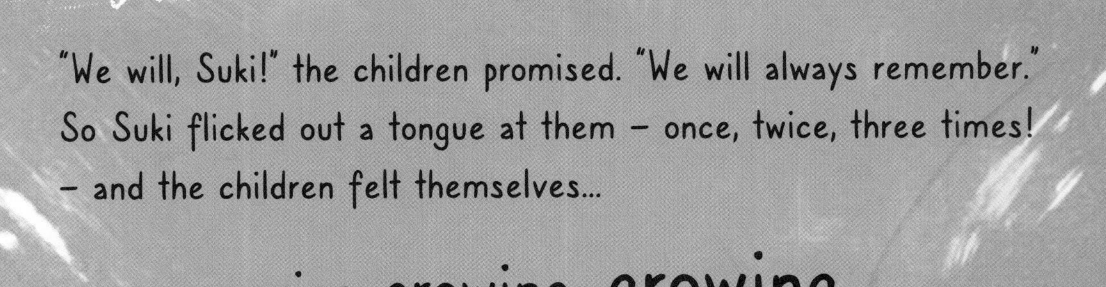

"We will, Suki!" the children promised. "We will always remember."
So Suki flicked out a tongue at them – once, twice, three times!
– and the children felt themselves...

growing, growing, growing...

...until they were their full-size human selves again. They ran straight up the hill to find Mamgu.

"Mamgu, did you miss us?" they said. "We've been gone for ages!"

JUNO

"You've only been down by the fountain for a few minutes," Mamgu laughed as she pulled a tray of warm biscuits out of the oven.

The children told her all about their adventures while they gobbled up the biscuits.

"Well, isn't that amazing," said Mamgu. "The world is very full of magic, if you just know where to look."

How to find Your Own Magic Garden

Here is a treasure map that will help you to find your own Magic Garden.

Step 1. Go outside. This is where the magic happens. Go on a finding adventure!

Step 2. Look. If you just open your eyes, you will see that Nature is all around you – a dandelion growing up through the cracks in the pavement, a spider spinning a web in the corner of the window, little bugs scooting around in a puddle. Use your other senses – smell, feel, listen. Don't taste anything unless an adult tells you that it's safe!

Step 3. Gather. If you are careful and respectful, only taking things that you are allowed to or where there are many of them, you can bring a few natural treasures back inside with you.

Step 4. Create. In the Magic Garden, Nature wants you to play, just like you would play ball – back and forth!

What can you make, inspired by the treasures that you find in nature? Can you paint, write, draw something?

Can you write a story about what you find? Can you do a dance, or make a puppet show? Can you plant a tomato seed and water the little plant that grows? Show Nature that you appreciate the treasures you have been given!

Shann Jones

Shann Jones MBE (Mamgu) is a grandmother in real life, and wrote this story for her real-life grandchildren Macsen, Elis and Isabella. Shann has been a radio talk show host and newspaper journalist in America.

Today she lives with her husband, Rich, and their grown-up children on a goat farm overlooking the sea, where they all work together at their family business, Chuckling Goat. Shann loves to spend time in the real Magic Garden, and looks out for Suki's frog spawn every spring.

Hannah Rounding

Hannah is an artist, illustrator and community worker based a couple of miles down the coast from Shann.

The illustrations in this book have been created through a multi-media layering approach. Hannah has used printmaking and painting techniques to create the backgrounds, layered up with paper and digital collage and finished off with a combination of hand and digital drawings. The images are based upon Mamgu's real-life garden with a splash of inspiration from Monet for the pond!

It just so happens that Hannah's favourite animals are frogs!

The Magic Garden Frog
Published in Great Britain in 2024 by Graffeg Limited.

Graffeg, 24 Stradey Park Business Centre, Mwrwg Road, Llangennech, Llanelli, Carmarthenshire, SA14 8YP, Wales, UK.
Tel: 01554 824000. www.graffeg.com.

A CIP Catalogue record for this book is available from the British Library.

The publisher acknowledges the financial support of the Books Council of Wales. www.gwales.com.

ISBN 9781802585353

1 2 3 4 5 6 7 8 9